The Frightful Ride
of Michael McMichael

BONNY BECKER

ILLUSTRATED BY
MARK FEARING

CANDLEWICK PRESS

'Twas the thirteenth of November, a stormy night,
when the Thirteen bus hove into sight.
Something about it didn't seem right . . .

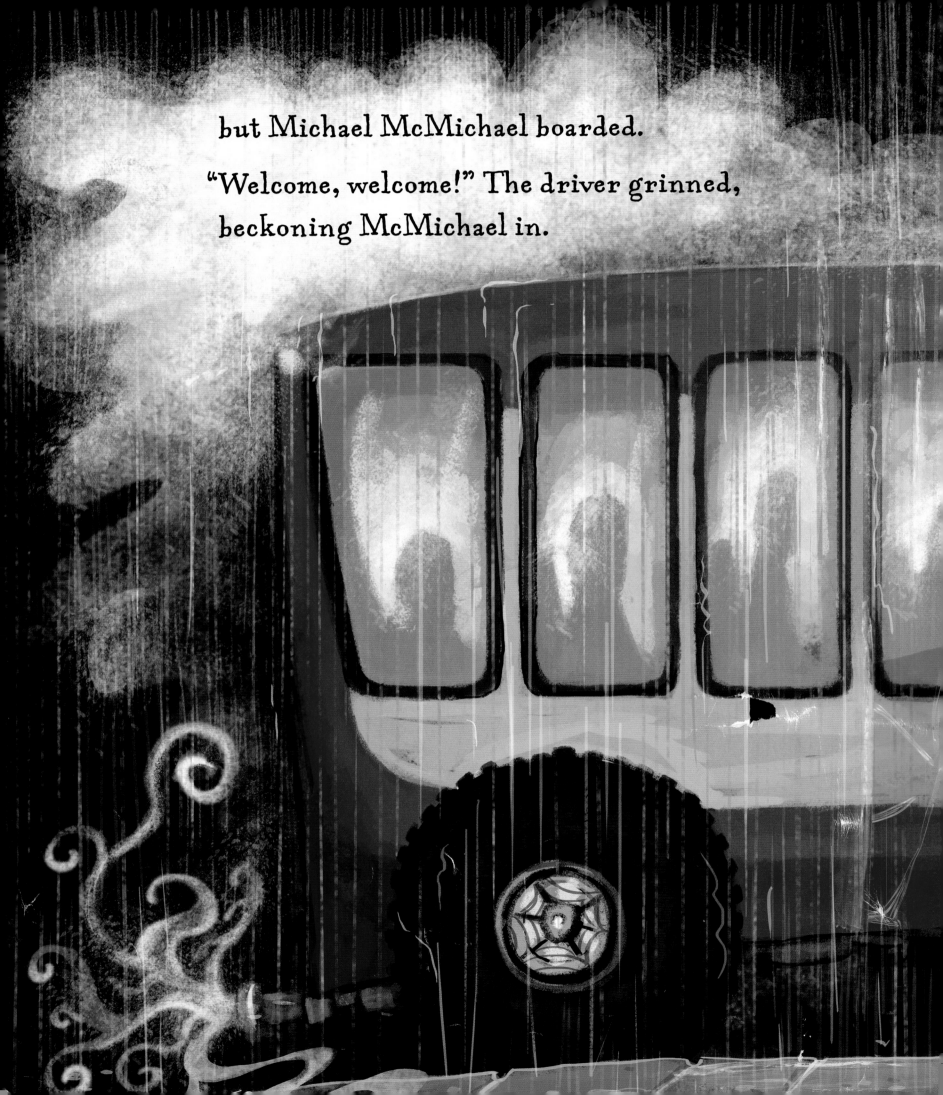

but Michael McMichael boarded.

"Welcome, welcome!" The driver grinned,
beckoning McMichael in.

His teeth were long and white as sin,
his nose bent and warted.

The bus was full, barely room inside.
Perhaps he should wait for a different ride?
But he was late. And, well, besides,
it was Gran's dear pet he transported.

So the bus slipped off on its late-night route
and Michael helped old ladies out
and, in general, was a lad most stout

as the riders steadily deboarded.

Soon there were five,

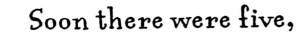

then two,

then one,

'til Michael McMichael was all alone
with a driver whose face was thin as bone
and more and more distorted!

When the bus was empty, no others in sight,
the driver hissed with soft delight.
"Doesn't the cold give an appetite
for body parts assorted?"

The boy, it seems, hadn't noticed before
the jaw-like opening of the door,

the tongue-like glisten of the floor,

the teeth-like seats it supported.

"Really, you should stop up here!
My grandmother's house is nearly near.
I bring her something very dear."
He held up the basket he sported.

"But you haven't paid," the driver moaned.
"I'm sorry to say you can't go home
'til you pay the fare with meat or bone.
Our coffers will not be shorted!"

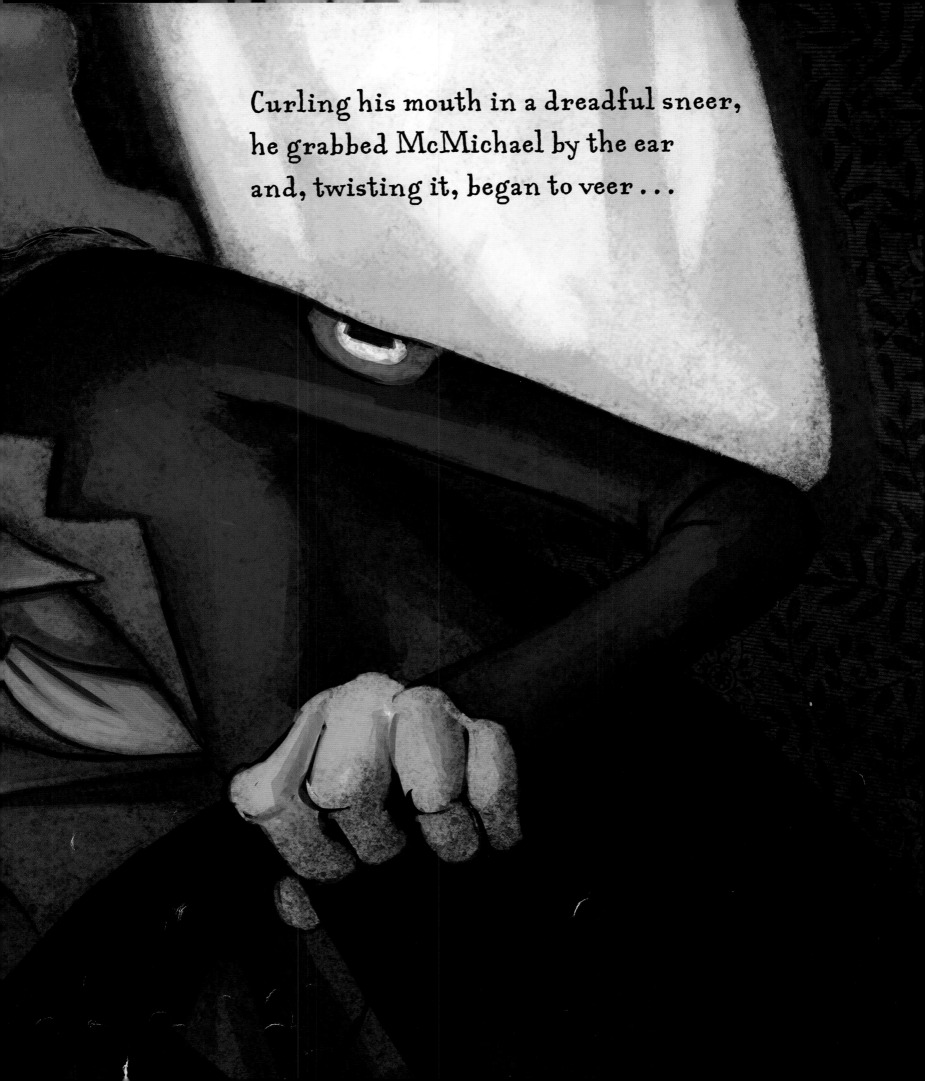

Curling his mouth in a dreadful sneer,
he grabbed McMichael by the ear
and, twisting it, began to veer . . .

toward a slathering maw most horrid!

Now, Michael was a peaceable boy,
kindness and cheer his greatest joys,
but the moment called for a desperate ploy
and to this the lad resorted.

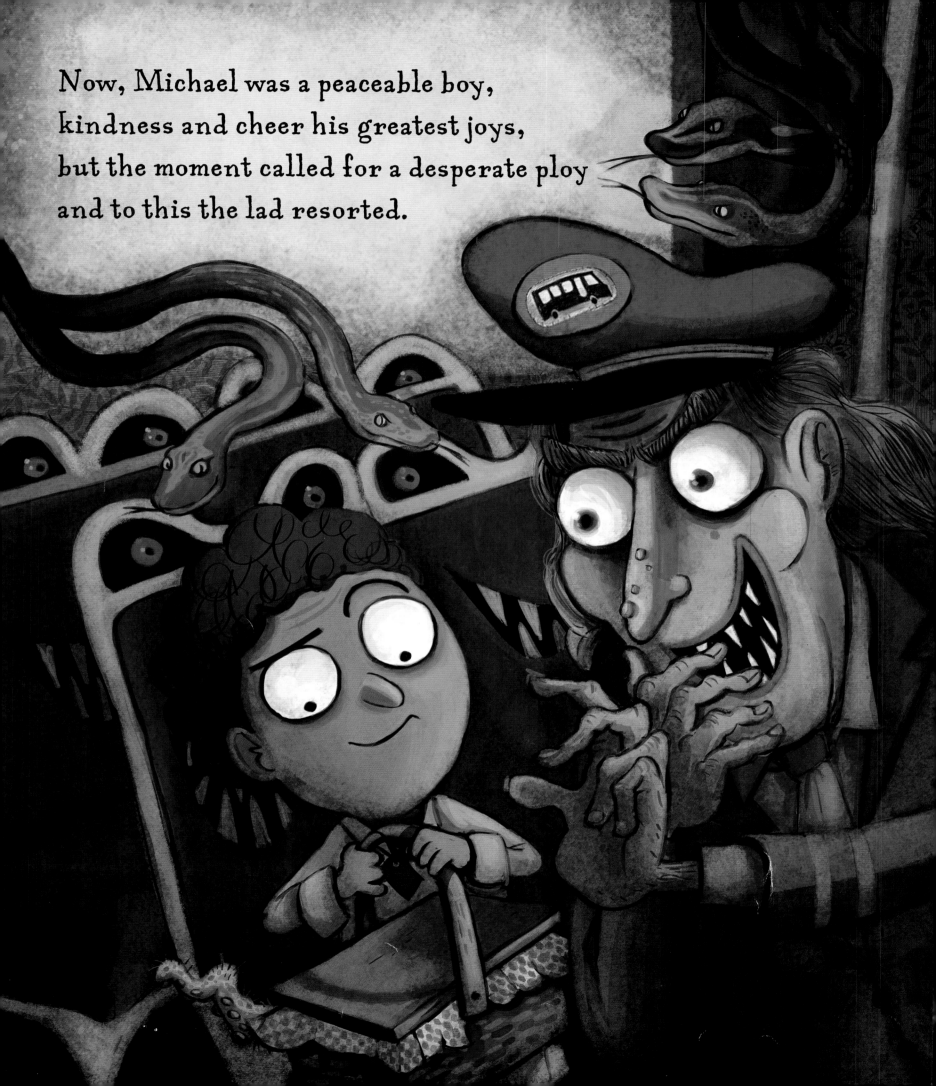

"Good sir," he cried. "Why the haste?
Should Gran's sweet thing go to waste?

Wouldn't you like just a little taste?
Your service should be rewarded."

McMichael lifted the basket lid —
in that darkness, something hid —
but the greedy driver did as bid.
His tongue uncoiled, black and contorted.

And thus, he met a terrible fate,
for his head and arms and legs were ate.
His shoes waved good-bye. So sad. Too late.
He was gone, moved on, exported.

'Twas the thirteenth of November, a stormy night,
when the Thirteen bus lurched off in fright
and Michael McMichael strolled out of sight.

Or so it's been reported.

For Miriam, fellow lover of words
B. B.

For Lily:
if it weren't for scary books,
she would never have learned to read
M. F.

Text copyright © 2018 by Bonny Becker
Illustrations copyright © 2018 by Mark Fearing

First edition 2018

Library of Congress Catalog Card Number pending
ISBN 978-0-7636-8150-0

18 19 20 21 22 23 TLF 10 9 8 7 6 5 4 3 2 1

Printed in Dongguan, Guangdong, China

This book was typeset in Aunt Mildred.
The illustrations were done as traditional pencil drawings and painted digitally.

Candlewick Press
99 Dover Street
Somerville, Massachusetts 02144

visit us at www.candlewick.com